HOOTS & TOOTS
& HAIRY BRUTES

The Continuing Adventures of Squib

Books in the Squib Series by Larry Shles

Moths & Mothers, Feathers & Fathers

Hoots & Toots & Hairy Brutes

Hugs & Shrugs

Aliens In My Nest

HOOTS & TOOTS & HAIRY BRUTES

The Continuing Adventures of Squib

Written and Illustrated by Larry Shles

JALMAR PRESS 1989

Jalmar Press
45 Hitching Post Drive, Bldg. 2
Rolling Hills Estates, CA 90274-4297

Library of Congress Cataloging-in-Publication Data

Shles, Larry.
Hoots & Toots & Hairy Brutes

Previously published under same title,
1st Ed. 1985

Summary: Troubled because he can only toot and not
hoot like other owls, Squib finally learns that
it is how one uses one's individual talents that makes
the difference.

[1. Fables.   2. Owls — Fiction.   3. Self-acceptance — Fiction]
I. Title.   II. Title: Hoots and toots and hairy brutes.
Library of Congress Catalog Card Number: 89-83466
ISBN 0-915190-56-7

Printed in the United States of America

Cloth   P   Pbk.   AL   10   9   8   7   6   5   4   3   2

To my daughter, Stacy, with much love
To Mahala Cox, whose elegant vision enriches the world
To Terry Cain, for invaluable guidance and faith

HOOTS & TOOTS
& HAIRY BRUTES

The Continuing Adventures of Squib

Squib was an unusually tiny owl

who couldn't hoot or fly.

Because of his problems, every owl ignored him.
Every day when he came home from his adventures,
Squib was eager to tell his parents about the amazing
things he'd seen.

"Mommy, you'll never guess what I saw this morning," Squib would toot. "I saw the strangest ants. They were carrying . . ."

"Hoot up, dear, I can hardly hear you," his mother would say.

Squib knew she wasn't really listening, but he tried again in his loudest toot. "I saw these weird ants . . ."

"I'm glad you did, dear," his mother would say as she continued with her chores.

Squib fared no better when he
went out to play with the other
young owls. The only time they let
Squib join in was when they
played owlpile.
Squib always wound up at the
bottom of the heap.

Nor would the owls make room for Squib around the campfire. Instead he would have to listen to their horror stories from the chilly shadows.

In these stories they whispered of the ugly and evil Hairy Brute and how he terrorized the forest. Without warning, loud explosions erupted from a stick he carried. Hundreds of forest animals had been injured or killed by the Brute.

"I know about the Hairy Brute, too," Squib tooted. But his tiny voice was swallowed by the darkness and the crackling of the fire.

Squib had already learned much about the Hairy Brute from his parents.

"He is so hideous, Squib," they would tell him. "He kills for no reason. You must always keep a keen eye out for him. And should you ever spot him, remain absolutely motionless and make no sound."

Squib began waking up in the middle of the night with terrible visions of the Brute.

One morning Squib was awakened by a sharp
explosion and the frantic hoots of his neighbors.
The Brute had attacked a young owl in the next
tree. Now no place in the forest was safe from the
ravages of the fiendish Brute.

But as Squib drew nearer to hear more, the
adult owls fell silent and moved away.

Denied any real details, Squib began painting pictures in his mind of what such a terrible monster might look like.

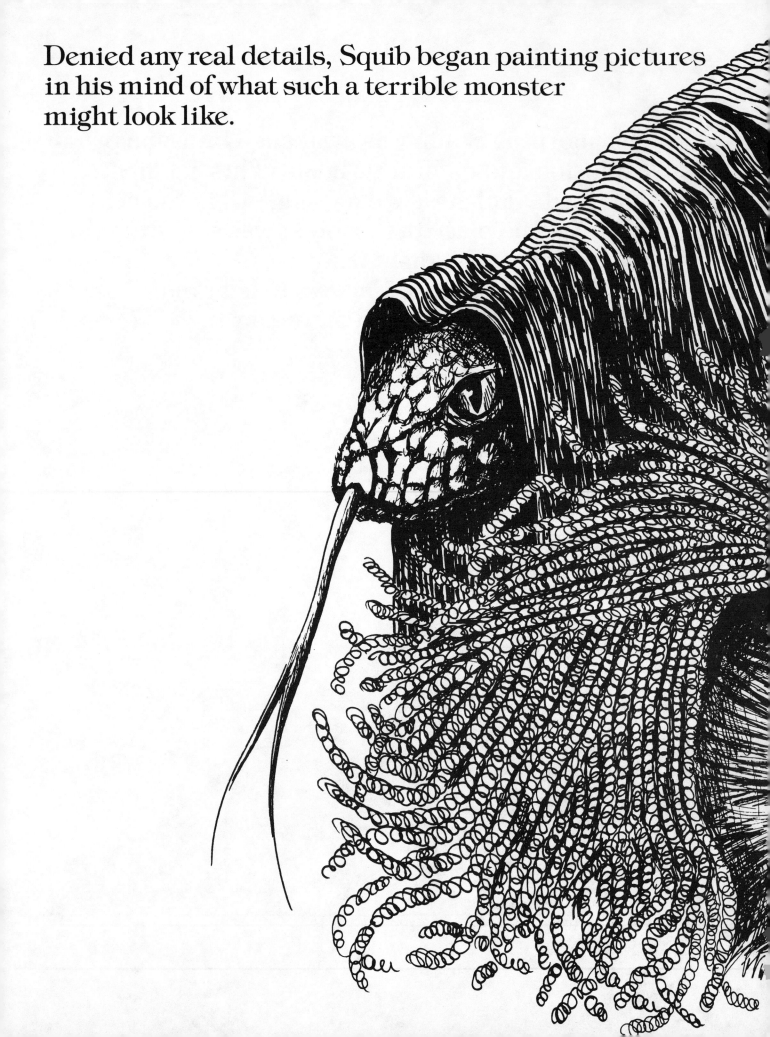

If only *I* were the Hairy Brute, Squib thought. I would be big, powerful, and feared. No one could ignore me then!

Half convinced that he *was* the Hairy Brute, Squib bombarded his elders with questions.

"Is the Brute a huge furry frog? Why can't he stay in his own forest? Dad, could you beat him up if he came to *our* nest?"

"Squib, when you're old enough to hoot, you'll be ready to understand such things," an adult would reply. "In the meantime, just hop off and play by yourself."

This attitude made Squib feel tinier than the tiny owl he already was.

After much thought, he came upon a solution to his problem. Since he could never be scary like the Brute, he'd have to learn how to hoot.

And when his toot became a hoot, everyone would listen to him.

Squib began practicing. He puffed out his chest,
thought HOOT!, and let it rip.
But it would come out as only a trivial *toot*.

toot

Squib tried to hoot on snoots and boots. He tried to hoot on fruits and newts. He even imagined hooting on the top of Hairy Brutes.

But all that ever came out was his weak,
pathetic
toot.

If only he could hoot like his father! When Dad lost his temper, he alerted the forest for miles around.

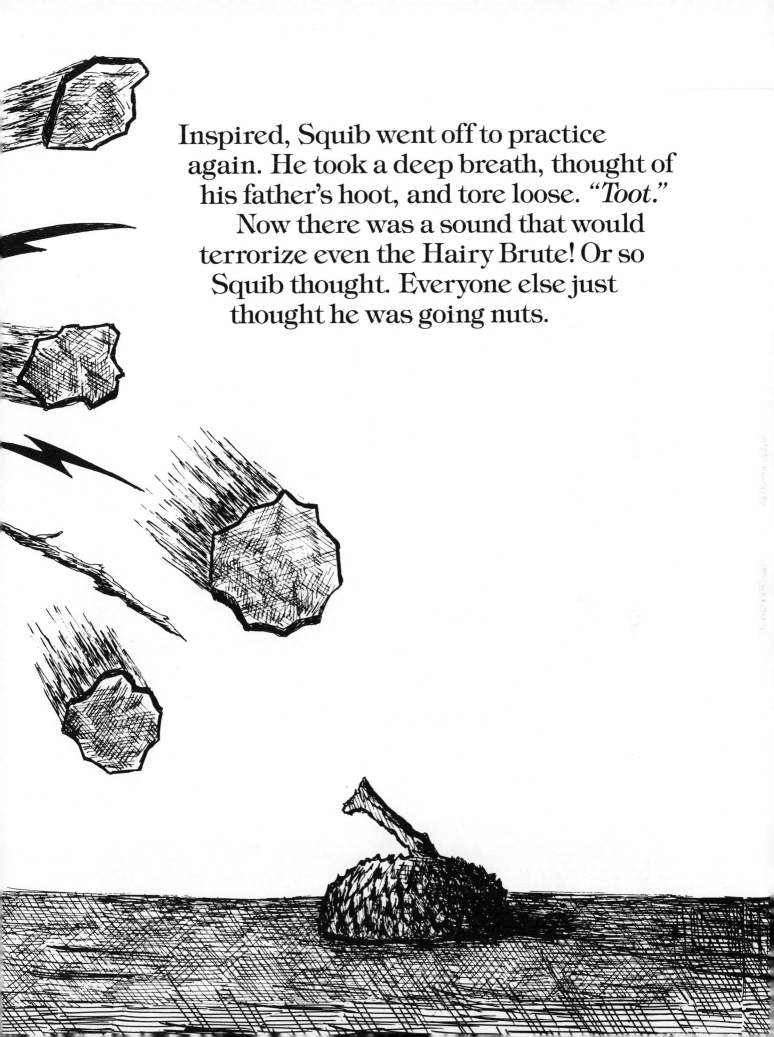

Inspired, Squib went off to practice again. He took a deep breath, thought of his father's hoot, and tore loose. *"Toot."* Now there was a sound that would terrorize even the Hairy Brute! Or so Squib thought. Everyone else just thought he was going nuts.

The harder he tried, the more surprising the results became. Squib's *toots* were turning into *moos, oinks, caws, snorts, ribbits, peeps,* and *neighs.*

Embarrassed, he'd look around, hoping no one had heard him.

Deciding he just didn't give a hoot, Squib turned into a pest. He snuck up on a sleeping cat, perched on his ear, and unleashed his mightiest *toot*. The cat didn't even open an eye.

He crept up on a blue jay, perched on a branch, and let out a sudden *toot*. The blue jay, irritated, unleashed a screech that blasted Squib off the branch.

Totally dejected, Squib went to his mother. "I want to be able to hoot, Mom," he said in a very whiny *toot*.

His mother, seeing how miserable Squib was, made appointments with experts to determine why he was hootless.

The orthodontist was certain that Squib's problem was the result of overbeak. Squib was fitted for braces and headgear.

Once the braces were removed, Squib again tried to hoot. Concentrating on changing the "t" sound to an "h" sound, he mumbled his new word. It was strange. The "t" and "h" had now merged. Squib's first sound after his braces came off was *"thooth."*

Next Squib's mother took him to a psychowlogist. "This youngster is too tense to hoot," he exclaimed. Squib was instructed to breathe deeply and repeat the sound "Owlmmmmmmmm" over and over again.

Squib formed his relaxed beak into an "oo" shape and calmly breathed out the sound he hoped would be his first hoot.

Well, it wasn't. And it wasn't a toot, either. His new sound was *"shoosh."* Squib was too relaxed now to even give a toot.

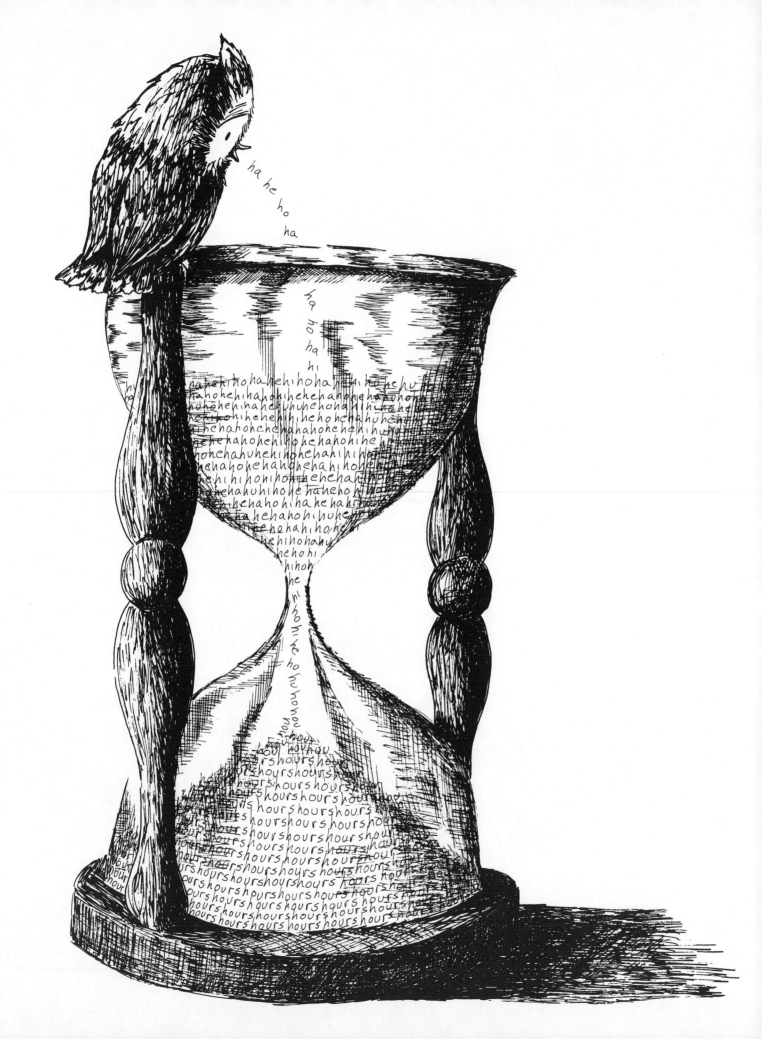

As a last resort, Squib's mother hired a tutor to teach him. At first Squib was confused. He could already toot. Why did he need a tooter? And if a tutor taught hooting, certainly she should be called a hooter rather than a tooter.

Once this confusion was settled, Squib's hoot tutor, who was cuter and astuter than most hooters, launched him into his lessons. Squib was instructed to practice all his "h" sounds:

ho-ho-he-he-hi-hi-huh-huh-ha-ha-ha-ha.........hah! The hoot tutor called Squib's family together to hear her student's progress. All eyes were on Squib as he was placed center branch. Clearing his throat and looking skyward, he meekly brought forth his new sound.

Before he could even hear what he had said, all his relatives were laughing. Squib spoke again. The laughter was louder. And no wonder. *Froot* was his new sound. *"Froot"?* The tutor had done nothing more than turn Squib into a frooty tutee.

HO

HAH

HAH HAH

HAH HAH

HAH

HAH

HAH

HAH

HAH

HAH

HAH

HAH

HAH

YUK

HAH

HAH

HAH

HAH

HAH

HAH HAH HAH

HO

HAH

HAH

HAH

HAH HAH

HAH

HAH

HAH

HAH

HAH

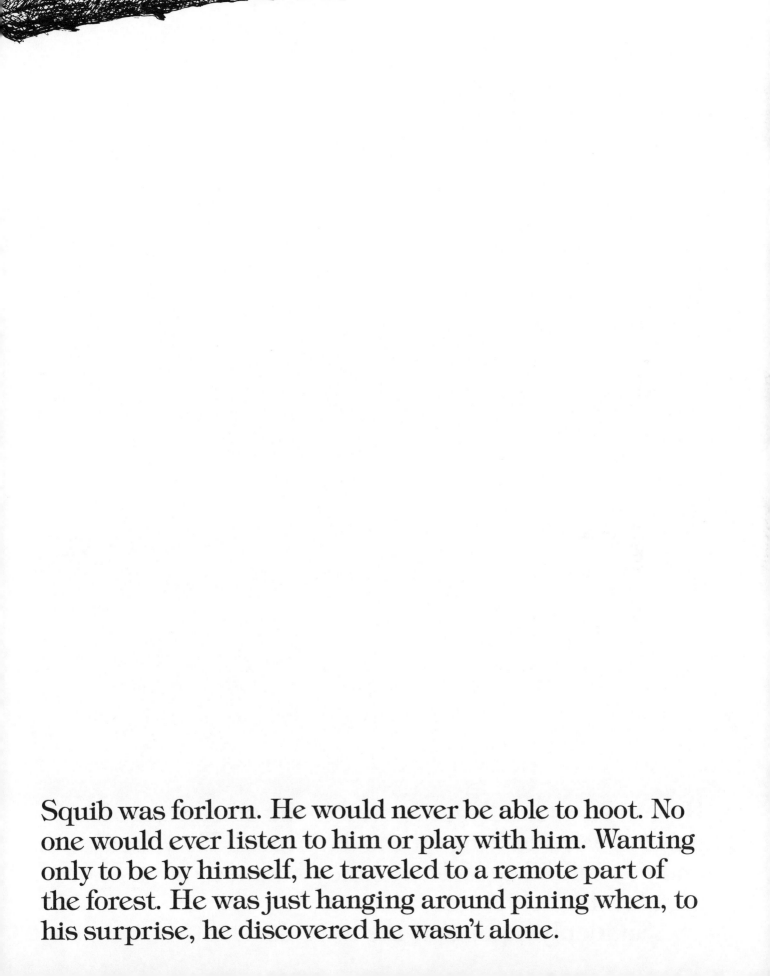

Squib was forlorn. He would never be able to hoot. No one would ever listen to him or play with him. Wanting only to be by himself, he traveled to a remote part of the forest. He was just hanging around pining when, to his surprise, he discovered he wasn't alone.

He had accidentally journeyed to the place where his parents were hunting for the day's meal. How regal and powerful they looked as they scanned the distant meadow for field mice.

Suddenly Squib saw the terrible beast.

The gigantic creature had loomed up just a short distance from him. It was the Hairy Brute. He was poised, staring at Squib's mother and father, and pointing an ugly-looking stick at them.

Squib realized the lives of his parents were at stake. His heart began to pound; his wing tips went stiff; his toes curled up from fright. He had to warn them immediately, but he knew the only thing they could hear at that distance would be a mighty hoot.

Please, God, let this be a hoot. Please!

Squib concentrated as hard as he could, opened his tiny beak wide, and let out his warning.......

"*Toot!*"

.......It was still a toot—but the most remarkable toot you'd ever want to hear. It wasn't loud, but it was crystal clear and pure.

Like a swift arrow, Squib's toot flew across the meadow, alerting his parents. Startled to hear such a beautiful sound, they looked around and discovered the Hairy Brute. Instantly they flew off the branch. The Brute's shot rang out. Too late! Squib's parents had soared to safety.

From that moment on, Squib found that his life was changed. All his struggle and practice trying to hoot had created a toot that was unique. And once he realized the value of his tiny yet beautiful toot, Squib stood prouder. The young owls now invited him to join in all their games. And when they played owlpile, Squib would wind up on the top of the heap.

Now when Squib tooted around a sleeping cat, cats from all over the neighborhood would awaken.

They would converse

with him for hours about their day's adventures.

Within the campfire circle, Squib now had his own Hairy Brute story to tell. Everyone listened intently and asked him many questions when he finished.

Squib now knew that his toot could be worth as much as any hoot in the world.

The Continuing Saga of Squib the Owl

"Shles has caught the spirit of the fledgling...an extremely effective portrayal of the child we all once were. Bravo to him for giving us Squib — long may he live and grow!" — **Doris Weber, St. Louis Globe-Democrat.**

"Squib allows readers to be vulnerable and invites them to trust, to dare, and to triumph." — **Marian Junge, Teacher and Librarian.**

Moths & Mothers, Feathers & Fathers
A Story About a Tiny Owl Named Squib

Larry Shles

Squib is a tiny owl who cannot hoot or fly, neither can he understand his feelings. He must face the frustration, fear, and loneliness that we all must face at different times in our lives. Struggling with these feelings, he searches, at least, for understanding.

8 1/2 x 11, 72 pages, paperback, illustrations.
ISBN 0-915190-57-5 $7.95

Aliens In My Nest
Squib Meets the Teen Creature

Larry Shles

In *Aliens in my Nest*, Squib comes home from summer camp to find that his older brother, Andrew, has turned into a snarly, surly, defiant, and non-communicative adolescent. Friends, temperament, dress, entertainment, thoughts about authority, room decor, eating habits, music likes and dislikes, isolation, internal and external conflict and many other areas of change are dealt with in this remarkably illustrated book.

8 1/2 x 11, 80 pages, trade paperback, illustrations.
ISBN 0-915190-49-4 $7.95

Jalmar Press.

Hoots & Toots & Hairy Brutes
The Continuing Adventures of Squib

Larry Shles

Squib — who can only toot — sets out to learn how to give a mighty hoot. His attempts result in abject failure. Every reader who has struggled with life's limitations will recognize his struggles and triumphs in the microcosm of Squib's forest world. A parable for all ages from eight to eighty.

8 1/2 x 11, 72 pages, paperback, illustrations.
ISBN 0-915190-56-7 $7.95

Hugs & Shrugs
The Continuing Saga of Squib

Larry Shles

Squib feels incomplete. He has lost a piece of himself. He searches everywhere only to discover that his missing piece has fallen in and not out. He becomes complete again once he discovers his own inner-peace.

8 1/2 x 11, 72 pages, trade paperback.
ISBN 0-915190-47-8 $7.95

Jalmar Press.

Learning The Skills of Peacemaking
An Activity Guide for Elementary-Age Children

"Global peace begins with you. Guide develops this fundamental concept in fifty lessons. If this curriculum was a required course in every elementary school in every country, we would see world peace in our children's lifetimes." — *Letty Cottin Pogrebin*, Ms. Magazine
0-915190-46-X $21.95
8½ × 11   paperback, illus.

Project Self-Esteem EXPANDED
A Parent Involvement Program for Elementary-Age Children

An innovative parent-support program that promotes children's self-worth. "Project Self Esteem is the most extensively tested and affordable drug and alcohol preventative program available."

0-915190-59-1 $39.95
8½ × 11   paperback, illus.

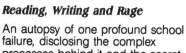

The Two Minute Lover
Announcing A New Idea In Loving Relationships

No one is foolish enough to imagine that s/he *automatically* deserves success. Yet, almost everyone thinks that they automatically deserve sudden and continuous success in marriage. Here's a book that helps make that belief a reality.
0-915190-52-4 $9.95
6 × 9   paperback, illus.

Reading, Writing and Rage

An autopsy of one profound school failure, disclosing the complex processes behind it and the secret rage that grew out of it.

Must reading for anyone working with learning disabled, functional illiterates, or juvenile delinquents.

0-915190-42-7 $16.95
5½ × 8½   paperback

Feel Better Now
30 Ways to Handle Frustrations in Three Minutes or Less

A practical menu of instant stress reduction techniques, designed to be used right in the middle of high-pressure situations. Feel Better Now includes stress management tools for every problem and every personality style.
0-915190-66-4 $9.95
6 × 9 paperback, appendix, biblio.

Esteem Builders

You CAN improve your students' behavior and achievement through building self-esteem. Here is a book packed with classroom- proven techniques, activities, and ideas you can immediately use in your own program or at home.

Ideas, ideas, ideas, for grades K-8 and parents.

0-915190-53-2 $39.95
8½ × 11   paperback, illus.

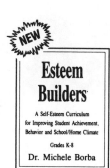

Good Morning Class—I Love You!
Thoughts and Questions About Teaching from the Heart

A book that helps create the possibility of having schools be places where students, teachers and principals get what every human being wants and needs—LOVE!

0-915190-58-3 $6.95
5½ × 8½ paperback, illus.

I am a blade of grass
A Breakthrough in Learning and Self-Esteem

Help your students become "lifetime learners," empowered with the confidence to make a positive difference in their world (without abandoning discipline or sacrificing essential skill and content acquisition).
0-915190-54-0 $14.95
6 × 9   paperback, illus.

Unlocking Doors to Self-Esteem

Presents innovative ideas to make the secondary classroom a more positive learning experience—socially and emotionally—for students and teachers. Over 100 lesson plans included. Designed for easy infusion into curriculum. Gr. 7-12

0-915190-60-5 $16.95
6 × 9 paperback, illus

SAGE: *Self-Awareness Growth Experiences*

A veritable treasure trove of activities and strategies promoting positive behavior and meeting the personal/social needs of young people in grades 7-12. Organized around affective learning goals and objectives. Over 150 activities.
0-915190-61-3   **$16.95**
6 × 9 paperback, illus.

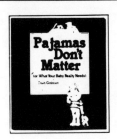

Pajamas Don't Matter:
(or What Your Baby Really Needs)

Here's help for new parents everywhere! Provides valuable information
and needed reassurances to new
parents as they struggle through the
frantic, but rewarding, first years of
their child's life.
0-915190-21-4 $5.95
8½ × 11   paperback, full color

Why Does Santa Celebrate Christmas?

What do wisemen, shepherds and
angels have to do with Santa,
reindeer and elves? Explore this
Christmas fantasy which ties all of
the traditions of Christmas into one
lovely poem for children of all
ages.
0-915190-67-2 $12.95
8 1/2 x 11 hardcover, full color

Feelings Alphabet

Brand-new kind of alphabet book full
of photos and word graphics that will
delight readers of all ages.''. . .lively,
candid. . .the 26 words of
this pleasant book express
experiences common to all children.''
Library Journal
0-935266-15-1 $7.95
6 × 9   paperback, B/W photos

The Parent Book

A functional and sensitive guide for
parents who want to enjoy every min-
ute of their child's growing years.
Shows how to live with children in
ways that encourage healthy emo-
tional development. Ages 3-14.
0-915190-15-X $9.95
8½ × 11   paperback, illus.

Aliens In My Nest
SQUIB Meets The Teen Creature

Squib comes home from summer
camp to find that his older brother,
Andrew, has turned into a snarly,
surly, defiant, and non-communicative adolescent. *Aliens* explores the
effect of Andrew's new behavior on
Squib and the entire family unit.
0-915190-49-4 $7.95
8½ × 11   paperback, illus.

Hugs & Shrugs
The Continuing Saga of SQUIB

Squib feels incomplete. He has lost a
piece of himself. He searches every
where only to discover that his missing piece has fallen in and not out.
He becomes complete again once
he discovers his own inner-peace.

0-915190-47-8 $7.95
8½ × 11   paperback, illus.

Moths & Mothers/
Feather & Fathers
*A Story About a Tiny Owl
Named SQUIB*

Squib is a tiny owl who cannot fly.
Neither can he understand his feelings. He must face the frustration,
grief, fear, guilt and loneliness that
we all must face at different times in
our lives. Struggling with these feelings, he searches, at least, for
understanding.

0-915190-57-5 $7.95
8½ × 11   paperback, illus.

Hoots & Toots & Hairy Brutes
*The Continuing Adventures
of SQUIB*

Squib—who can only toot—sets out
to learn how to give a mighty hoot.
His attempts result in abject failure.
Every reader who has struggled with
life's limitations will recognize their
own struggles and triumphs in the
microcosm of Squib's forest world. A
parable for all ages from 8 to 80.

0-915190-56-7 $7.95
8½ × 11   paperback, illus.

Do I Have To Go To School Today?
Squib Measures Up!

Squib dreads the daily task of going
to school. In this volume, he
daydreams about all the reasons he
has not to go. But, in the end, Squib
convinces himself to go to school
because his teacher accepts him
''Just as he is!''

0-915190-62-1 $7.95
8½ × 11   paperback, illus.

The Turbulent Teens
Understanding Helping Surviving

''This book should be read by every
parent of a teenager in America. . .It
gives a parent the information
needed to understand teenagers and
guide them wisely.''—Dr. Fitzhugh
Dodson, author of *How to Parent,
How to Father, and How to Discipline
with Love.*
0-913091-01-4 $8.95
6 × 9   paperback.

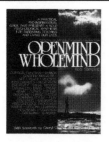

Openmind/Wholemind
Parenting & Teaching Tomorrow's Children Today

A book of powerful possibilities that honors the capacities, capabilities, and potentials of adult and child alike. Uses Modalities, Intelligences, Styles and Creativity to explore how the brain-mind system acquires, processes and expresses experience. Foreword by M. McClaren & C. Charles.
0-915190-45-1 $14.95
7 × 9   paperback
81 B/W photos   29 illus.

Present Yourself! *Captivate Your Audience With Great Presentation Skills*

Become a presenter who is a dynamic part of the message. Learn about Transforming Fear, Knowing Your Audience, Setting The Stage, Making Them Remember and much more. Essential reading for anyone interested in the art of communication. Destined to become the standard work in its field.
0-915190-51-6   paper $9.95
0-915190-50-8   cloth $18.95
6 × 9   paper/cloth. illus.

Unicorns Are Real
A Right-Brained Approach to Learning

Over 100,000 sold. The long-awaited "right hemispheric" teaching strategies developed by popular educational specialist Barbara Vitale are now available. Hemispheric dominance screening instrument included.
0-915190-35-4 $12.95
8½ × 11   paperback, illus.

Unicorns Are Real Poster

Beautifully-illustrated. Guaranteed to capture the fancy of young and old alike. Perfect gift for unicorn lovers, right-brained thinkers and all those who know how to dream. For classroom, office or home display.

JP9027 $4.95
19 × 27   full color

Imagination is the unicorn that lifts us above the mundane chains that bind the minds of many and flies us on fantastic wings to a place where dreams DO come true.

Metaphoric Mind (Revised Ed.)
Here is a plea for a balanced way of thinking and being in a culture that stands on the knife-edge between catastrophe and transformation. The metaphoric mind is asking again, quietly but insistently, for equilibrium. For, after all, equilibrium is the way of nature.
0-915190-68-0 $14.95
7 x 10 paperback, B/W photos

Don't Push Me, I'm Learning as Fast as I Can

Barbara Vitale presents some remarkable insights on the physical growth stages of children and how these stages affect a child's ability, not only to learn, but to function in the classroom.
JP9112 $12.95
Audio Cassette

Tapping Our Untapped Potential

This Barbara Vitale tape gives new insights on how you process information. Will help you develop strategies for improving memory, fighting stress and organizing your personal and professional activities.

JP9111 $12.95
Audio Cassette

Free Flight *Celebrating Your Right Brain*

Journey with Barbara Vitale, from her uncertain childhood perceptions of being "different" to the acceptance and adult celebration of that difference. A book for right-brained people in a left-brained world. Foreword by Bob Samples.
0-915190-44-3 $9.95
5½ × 8½   paperback, illus.

"He Hit Me Back First"
Self-Esteem through Self-Discipline

Simple techniques for guiding children toward self-correcting behavior as they become aware of choice and their own inner authority.
0-915190-36-2 $12.95
8½ × 11   paperback, illus.

Learning To Live, Learning To Love

An inspirational message about the importance of love in everything we do. Beautifully told through words and pictures. Ageless and timeless.
0-915190-38-9 $7.95
6 × 9   paperback, illus.

TA For Tots
(and other prinzes)

Over 500,000 sold.

This innovative book has helped thousands of young children and their parents to better understand and relate to each other. Ages 4-9.
0-915190-12-5 $12.95
8½ × 11   paper, color, illus.

TA For Tots, Vol. II

Explores new ranges of feelings and suggests solutions to problems such as feeling hurt, sad, shy, greedy, or lonely.

Ages 4-9.

0-915190-25-7 $12.95
8½ × 11   paper, color, illus.

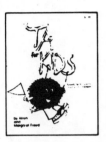

TA for Kids
(and grown-ups too)

Over 250,000 sold.

The message of TA is presented in simple, clear terms so youngsters can apply it in their daily lives. Warm Fuzzies abound. Ages 9-13.
0-915190-09-5 $9.95
8½ × 11   paper, color, illus.

TA For Teens
(and other important people)

Over 100,000 sold.

Using the concepts of Transactional Analysis. Dr. Freed explains the ups and downs of adulthood without talking down to teens. Ages 13-18.
0-915190-03-6 $18.95
8½ × 11   paperback, illus.

Original Warm Fuzzy Tale *Learn about "Warm Fuzzies" firsthand.*

Over 100,000 sold.

A classic fairytale...with adventure, fantasy, heroes, villains and a moral. Children (and adults, too) will enjoy this beautifully illustrated book.

0-915190-08-7 $7.95
6 × 9   paper, full color, illus.

Songs of The Warm Fuzzy
"All About Your Feelings"

The album includes such songs as Hitting is Harmful, Being Scared, When I'm Angry, Warm Fuzzy Song, Why Don't Parents Say What They Mean, and I'm Not Perfect (Nobody's Perfect).
JP9003 $12.95
          Cassette

Tot Pac *(Audio-Visual Kit)*

Includes 5 filmstrips, 5 cassettes, 2 record LP album. A *Warm Fuzzy I'm OK* poster, 8 coloring posters, 10 Warm Fuzzies. 1 *TA for Tots* and 92 page *Leader's Manual*. No prior TA training necessary to use Tot Pac in the classroom! Ages 2-9.
JP9032 $150.00
Multimedia program

Kid Pac *(Audio-Visual Kit)*

Teachers, counselors, and parents of pre-teens will value this easy to use program. Each *Kid Pac* contains 13 cassettes, 13 filmstrips, 1 *TA For Kids*, and a comprehensive *Teacher's Guide*, plus 10 Warm Fuzzies. Ages 9-13.
JP9033 $195.00
Multimedia Program

B.L. Winch & Assoc./Jalmar Press
45 Hitching Post Dr., Bldg. 2
Rolling Hills Estates, CA 90274

CALL TOLL FREE: 800/662-9662
In California, Call Collect: 213/547-1240

Please Enclose Check or Credit Card Information

NAME

STREET ADDRESS OR R.F.D.

CITY/STATE/ZIP

☐ Charge to VISA/MC   ☐ Acct. # _____   Exp. Date _____

Cardholder's Signature _____

TITLE	QTY	UNIT PRICE	TOTAL

Sub-Total: _____
CA Sales Tax: _____
Add 10% Shipping/Handling (**Min. $3.00**): _____
TOTAL: _____